HOW TO TRAIN YOUR DRAGON

Meet ... everyone from HOW TO TRAIN YOUR DRAGON

Stoick

This is **Stoick**. He is a Viking. The Vikings live on a small island.

Hiccup

This is **Hiccup**. His dad is Stoick.

Astrid

This is **Astrid**. She is Hiccup's friend.

These are **dragons**.
They come from
Dragon Island.

Toothless

This is **Toothless**.
He is a Night Fury.
He shoots fire.

The Red Death

The **Red Death** is a very big dragon.

Before you read ...

What do you think? Are the dragons good or bad?

New Words

What do these new words mean? Ask your teacher or use your dictionary.

fly

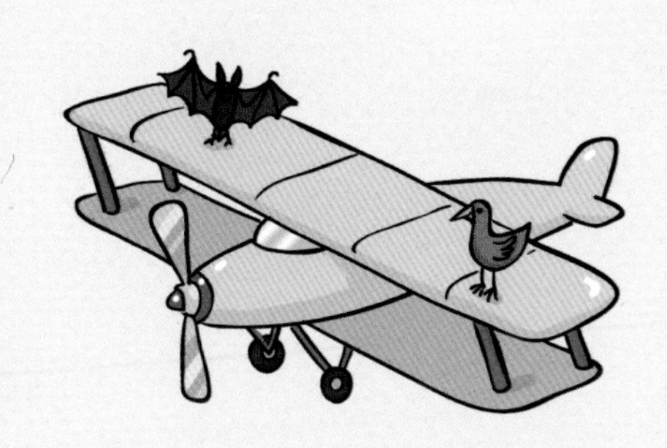

They can **fly**.

fight / fighter

The girls are **fighting**. They are good **fighters**.

frightened

The boy is **frightened**.

fire

The **fire** is hot.

help

He is **helping** his mother.

hit

The girl **hits** the ball. The ball **hits** the door.

tail

This cat has a long **tail**.

island

This is an **island**.

train

They are **training** the dogs.

shoot

'It's not true!'

CHAPTER ONE
Dragons in the night

The Vikings come from a small island. They are happy, but they have one big problem. Dragons live not very far away.

At night the dragons come. They fly away with the Vikings' animals.

The Vikings fight the dragons. Hiccup wants to fight too.

One night, Stoick sees Hiccup.

'What are you doing out of the house?' Stoick asks. He is angry.

'I want to fight dragons,' says Hiccup.

'No!' says Stoick. 'You are not a fighter. Go home!'

Hiccup does not go home. He looks up and he sees a dragon.

'It's a Night Fury!' he shouts.

Hiccup shoots and hits the dragon's tail. But Stoick does not see.

'Dad!' shouts Hiccup. 'I can fight dragons!'

Stoick does not answer.

'My dad doesn't listen to me,' Hiccup thinks.

CHAPTER TWO
How to train a dragon

In the morning, Hiccup looks for the Night Fury. He walks and walks.

Suddenly Hiccup sees the dragon. It can't fly. Hiccup is sad.

'I want to help you,' he says.

The Night Fury is angry. Hiccup is frightened but he looks into the dragon's eyes.

'You can't fly because of me,' says Hiccup. 'I can help you. I want to be your friend.'

Hiccup goes home. He does not talk to his dad about the Night Fury.

'I can make a new tail for the dragon,' he thinks.

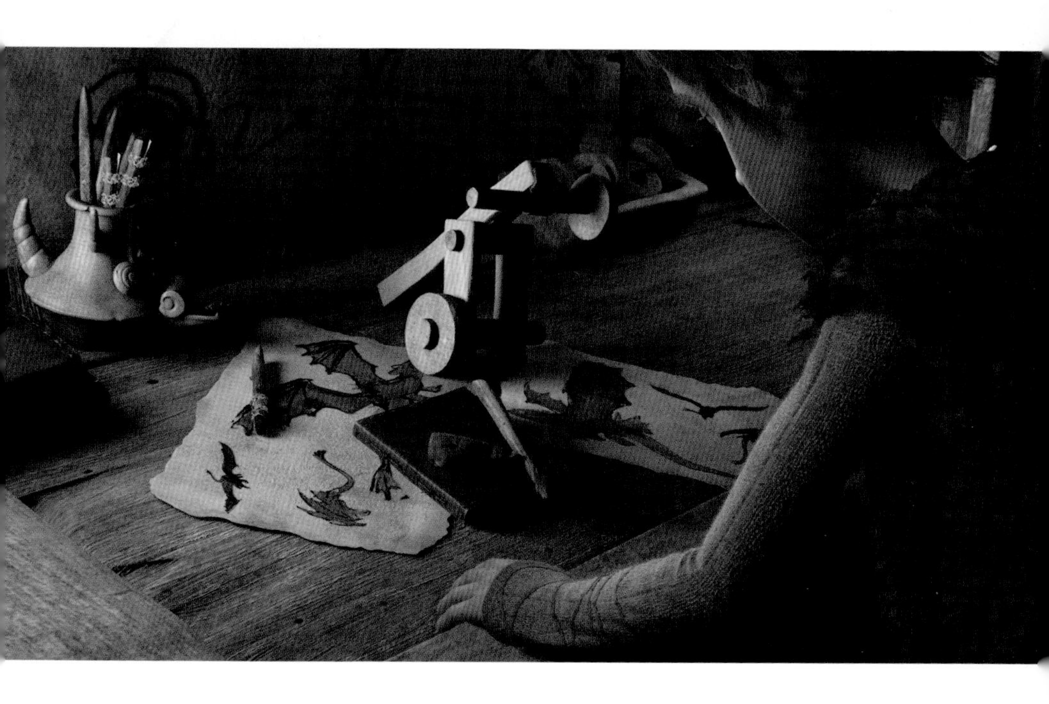

Hiccup goes to see the dragon again.
'Your name is Toothless,' he says.
He puts the new tail on Toothless.

Suddenly Toothless starts to fly with Hiccup.

'Wow!' shouts Hiccup. 'Let's go up, Toothless! Now let's go down!'

Hiccup laughs. 'I can train a dragon!' he says.

CHAPTER THREE
Dragon Island

Now Hiccup does not want to fight. He trains the dragons.

'How do you do that?' asks Astrid.

Hiccup does not answer.

'All dragons are bad,' says Astrid.

'It's not true!' thinks Hiccup.

One day, Astrid sees Hiccup with Toothless. She is angry. 'Good Vikings fight dragons,' she says.

'You don't understand,' answers Hiccup. 'Sit on Toothless. He's a friend.'

Astrid and Hiccup sit on Toothless.

'Wow! We're flying!' Astrid says. She is very happy.

Now she is not frightened of dragons.

Hiccup and Astrid see a lot of dragons. The dragons are flying to Dragon Island. Toothless flies there too.

On Dragon Island there is a very big and hungry dragon.

'Look!' says Astrid. 'It's the Red Death. It wants our animals. The Red Death is bad, not the dragons.'

CHAPTER FOUR
A good Viking

In the morning, Hiccup stands in front of all the Vikings.

'Can you fight a dragon?' asks Stoick. 'We want to see.'

But Hiccup does not fight. 'Dragons are friends,' he says. 'They can help Vikings.'

Stoick is very angry. 'No, you are not friends!' he says. 'Good Vikings fight dragons.'

'We're going to Dragon Island to stop all the dragons,' says Stoick.

'You don't understand,' says Hiccup. 'The Red Death is on the island.'

Stoick does not listen.

On Dragon Island the Vikings see the Red Death. They are very frightened.

Suddenly they see Hiccup. He is flying on Toothless!

'We can fight the Red Death!' shouts Hiccup.

Toothless and Hiccup fight the Red Death. The Red Death hits Hiccup with its tail.

'Hiccup!' shouts Stoick. He is frightened.

Toothless flies up. He shoots fire and stops the Red Death.

'You are a good Viking,' Stoick says to Hiccup. 'Now I understand. Dragons and Vikings are friends.'

THE END

DRAGON STORIES

There are a lot of stories about dragons. Some of the stories are very old.

In stories from China, dragons are good and help people. They can swim and they can make rain. People in China sometimes do a dragon dance.

In stories from the UK, dragons are sometimes bad. Dragons have wings and they can shoot fire. Sometimes they have two or three heads. In one old story, St George fights a dragon and helps a princess.

wing

There is a dragon in the book *The Hobbit*. The dragon's name is Smaug. It sleeps next to all its treasure.

ship

There are Viking stories about dragons too. Look at this Viking ship. Can you see the dragon?

What do these words mean? Find out.

story/stories people swim princess treasure

After you read

1 Complete the sentences with the words.

flying fight ~~help~~ puts shoots trains

a) Hiccup wants to ......help...... the Night Fury.
b) Hiccup .... a new tail on Toothless.
c) Hiccup .... dragons. They are his friends.
d) The Vikings see Hiccup. He is .... on Toothless.
e) Toothless .... a ball of fire.
f) Hiccup and Toothless .... the Red Death.

2 Read and circle.

a) *Astrid* / *Stoick* is Hiccup's friend.
b) *Stoick* / *Toothless* is Hiccup's dad.
c) Stoick does not listen to *Astrid* / *Hiccup*.
d) *Stoick* / *Hiccup* does not want to fight a dragon.
e) *Astrid* / *Stoick* flies with Hiccup and Toothless.

Where's the popcorn?
Look in your book.
Can you find it?

Puzzle time!

1 Dragons or Vikings? Complete the sentences.

a) There is a ....dragon.... on the red house.

b) There is one .... in the garden.

c) There are two .... in the sea.

d) Two .... are behind the blue house.

e) Three .... are in front of the school.

2 Find the words.

a) ....Viking....

b) ....

c) ....

d) ....

e) ....

3 Complete the sentences.

eyes four tails ~~two~~ two

This dragon is green and yellow.
It has ....two.... wings and two ....
It has .... heads and four ....
It has .... legs.

4 Draw your own dragon.

My dragon is ....
It has .... and ....
It has ....

Imagine ...

Work with a friend. Act out the scenes.

A

Astrid:	Good Vikings fight dragons.
Hiccup:	Not all dragons are bad. Sit on Toothless.
Astrid:	Wow! We're flying!
Hiccup:	Toothless is a friend.

B

Stoick:	Can you fight a dragon? We want to see.
Hiccup:	Dragons are friends.
Stoick:	No! Good Vikings fight dragons.
Hiccup:	You don't understand. Dragons can help Vikings.

Chant

1 Listen and read.

'Dragons aren't bad!'

The Vikings fight
The dragons in the night.

Then Hiccup says, 'Dad,
The dragons aren't bad.'

'They can help the Vikings,
They are good at fighting.'

Now Vikings play
With dragons in the day.

2 Say the chant.